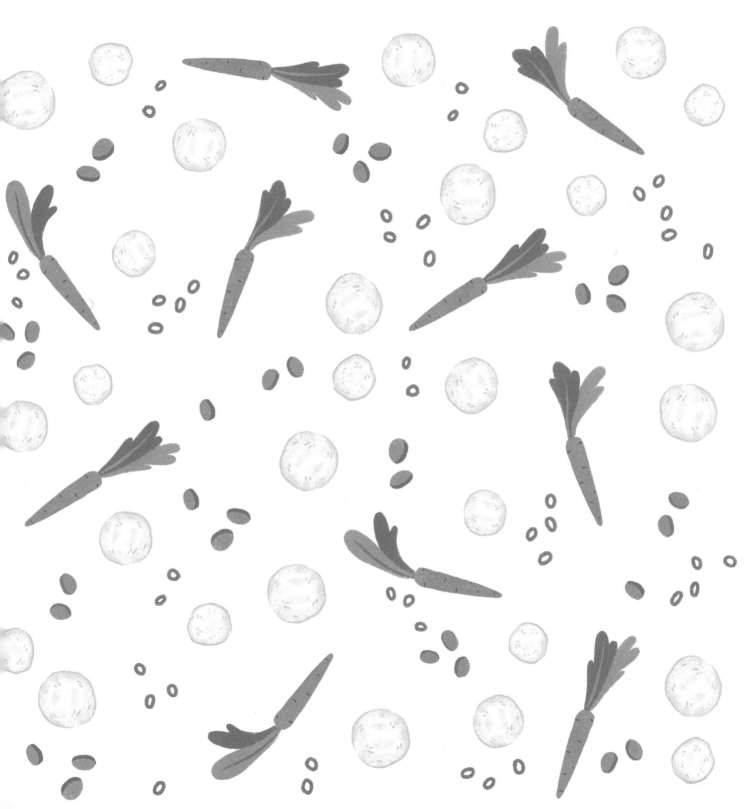

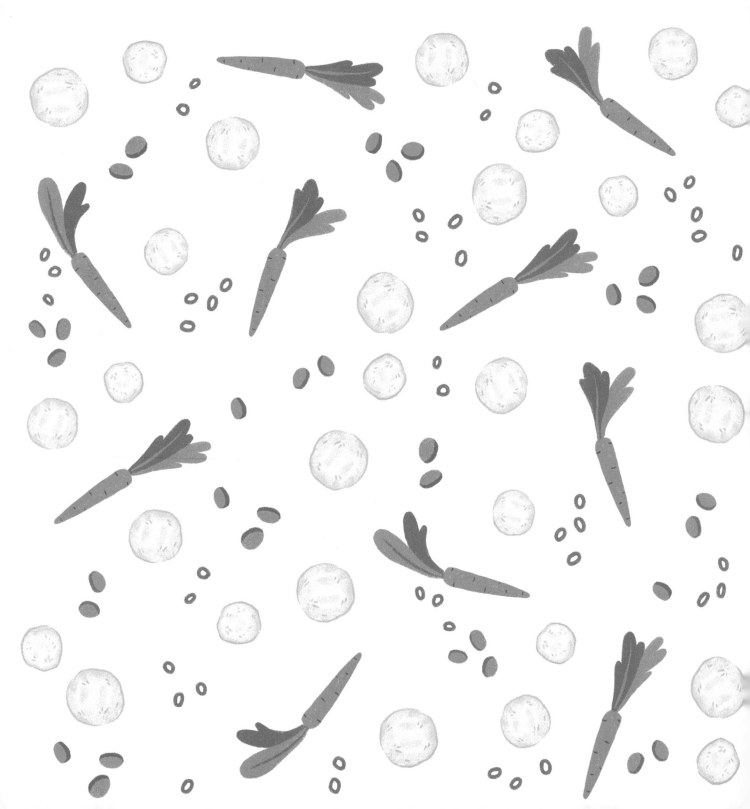

MATZO BALL-WONTON THANKSGIVING

Written By:
Amelie Suskind Liu
And
Leslie Lewinter-Suskind

Illustrated By:

Maria Dmitrieva

In Memory of Donald Chua Liu + Emilie Chua Liu

*I am Amelie Liu. This is my little brother, Asher. That's my
baby sister, Genevieve. And this is our dog, Max.
In a few days it will be my favorite holiday: Thanksgiving.
I'm so excited because my Nai Nai is coming all
the way from Taiwan to celebrate with us!*

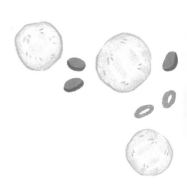

"Amelie, Asher, Genevieve," calls Daddy. "Nai Nai's here!"
Nai Nai calls me her "Little Shumai." Shumai is a kind of
dumpling. I don't know if I want to be a dumpling, but I know I
want to be Nai Nai's "Shumai!"

The next day, when I get home from school, the house is filled with
the most delicious smells and I know Nai Nai is cooking!

"Come, little Shumai," she says, "you will be my special taster.
I'm helping your mother prepare for Thanksgiving.
These delicious wontons are going into the soup."

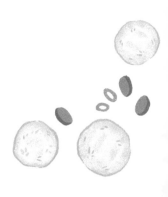

I start to explain that we can't have soup for
Thanksgiving. But, just as I open my mouth, she pops in
a delicious wonton.
Then the doorbell rings. I hear the kiss-kiss-kiss sound
that means Bubbe is here!

I start to explain that we can't have soup for
Thanksgiving. But, just as I open my mouth, she pops in
a delicious wonton.
Then the doorbell rings. I hear the kiss-kiss-kiss sound
that means Bubbe is here!

"Bubbe," I scream. Bubbe is my Mommy's mom.
"Bubbela," she says, as she kisses me. Bubbe kisses
Genevieve, Asher, Mommy, Daddy and even Max.
Then she sees Nai Nai and runs over to kiss her, too.

The next morning, Nai Nai and Bubbe
are talking about Thanksgiving.
I hear the word "soup." They are talking about whether
Matzo Ball or Wonton soup would be better at Thanksgiving dinner!

I can't believe it!

At first I am very quiet. Then I am very brave.
"There is no soup at Thanksgiving."

"Every year at our school," I tell them,
"we have a real Thanksgiving feast."

"All the kids bring real Thanksgiving food: there is turkey and
sweet potatoes and cranberry sauce and pumpkin pie.
No one has ever brought soup. Never!"

"We understand," say Nai Nai and Bubbe. "No soup."

I smile and go to school very happy.

After school, I race into the kitchen.
Bubbe and Nai Nai are both cooking.
Ooooo…it smells so, so, so yummy. I
can't wait to be the official taster!

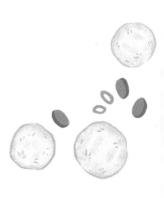

After school, I race into the kitchen.
Bubbe and Nai Nai are both cooking.
Ooooo…it smells so, so, so yummy. I
can't wait to be the official taster!

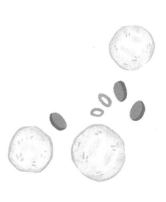

Bubbe pops a warm matzo ball into my mouth.
"So?" asks Bubbe.
"Mmmmmm!!! Delicious!!!" I say.

Then Nai Nai pops a steamy wonton into my mouth.
"Well?" asks Nai Nai.
"Mmmmmm!!! Yummy!!" I say.
"Is this what we're having for dinner?" I ask happily.

"No," says Bubbe. "THESE delicious matzo balls are
for Thanksgiving dinner tomorrow night."

"No, THESE delicious wontons are for Thanksgiving
dinner tomorrow night," says Nai Nai.

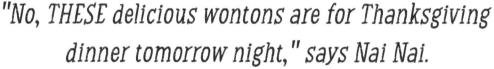

"No! No! No!" I scream.

"I told you. There is no soup on Thanksgiving!"

NO MATZO BALL SOUP!

NO WONTON SOUP!

NO SOUP ON THANKSGIVING!

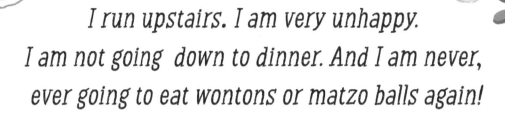

I run upstairs. I am very unhappy.
I am not going down to dinner. And I am never,
ever going to eat wontons or matzo balls again!

I hear a knock on my door. Bubbe and Nai Nai walk
in holding bowls of soup.

"Some of my melt-in-your-mouth matzo balls?" Bubbe asks.

"One of my light-as-a-cloud wontons?" asks Nai Nai.

"I am not hungry," I tell them in a strong voice.

I am VERY hungry. But I don't tell them that.

"Well, just in case." They put down the bowls of soup
and leave. My stomach is growling.

Now I am not only very unhappy with Bubbe and Nai Nai, I am very angry at Max.
But then...I get an idea!

Now I am not only very unhappy with
Bubbe and Nai Nai, I am very angry at
Max.
But then...I get an idea!

I know a way to make sure there is no soup for Thanksgiving.

Now I am very happy!

Oh no! Now I am not so happy.
But then I get another idea!

It looked so easy when
Bubbe and Nai Nai did it.

Suddenly, I hear a noise.
Bubbe and Nai Nai are standing in the doorway.

They don't look very happy.
In fact, they look a little bit mad.

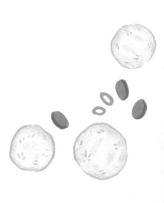

"My goodness!" say Bubbe and Nai Nai together.
Suddenly, Bubbe and Nai Nai begin to laugh.
They both wrap me up in their arms.
And then I get my best idea ever!

"This dining room looks so wonderful," Daddy says.
"And the food smells so delicious.
But the best thing about Thanksgiving is that we're all together."

I look at the buffet table. Turkey, sweet potatoes, cranberry sauce,
stuffing, and everything in-between: masala curry, collard greens,
couscous, Irish soda bread and some things I can't even name.
It all smells so good!

It makes me more than very hungry...
It makes me very, very happy!!!

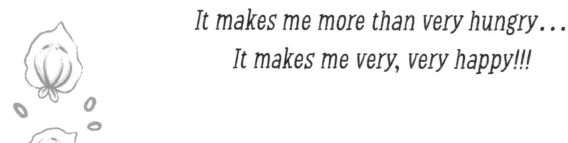

*Bubbe and Nai Nai bring
me my soup together. Then
they kiss me on the top of my head.
I look into my bowl.
Floating beautifully in the golden broth are a lovely
round matzo ball and a
fluffy white wonton, side-by-side like warm and loving friends.
I can't wait to taste them!*

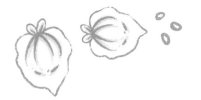

Author's Note

Like the character Amelie, Thanksgiving has always been my favorite holiday. As a little girl, I was torn between the two cultures of my family. All I wanted to have was a Thanksgiving with turkey, sweet potatoes, and definitely not matzo ball-wonton soup. Though I loved my Chinese and Jewish sides of the family, all I wanted was a real Thanksgiving. I would have done anything to suppress my identity in order to feel like a true American.

However, as I grew older I began to appreciate the beauty in my intertwined heritages. Rather than separating my cultures as I used to do with the food on my plate, I realized I should let them blend, mingle, and combine. The mixture of matzo ball and wonton soups makes for a scrumptious Thanksgiving meal.

It is my hope that kids like me feel pride in their perfectly blended cultures. When Thanksgiving time comes, I hope they jump in excitement as they help their relatives cook. I hope their hearts warm with happiness as they see their recipe of matzo ball-wonton soup served at Thanksgiving dinner.

Though my journey to seeing the beauty of my cultures may be quite different from yours, one thing holds true: Thanksgiving is a holiday of gratitude and appreciation. And, much like Amelie, America is a melting pot of heritages that should be celebrated. A real Thanksgiving reflects America as it is: matzo ball-wonton soup, masala curry, and Irish soda bread - not just turkey and potatoes. Next Thanksgiving, I challenge you to hold true to the traditions of the holiday, and give thanks to the cultures that make you, you.

About the Authors

Amelie Liu is a Chinese-Jewish 16-year-old born and raised in Chicago.
Amelie is a life-long writer and first began exploring her identity in a 5th-grade assignment
about the origins of her name. Though she has never published a book until now, Amelie has written
many pieces about her biracial identity. Notably, she published an op-ed titled "I'm a multicultural
teen trying to fit into our 'melting pot'" in the Chicago Tribune about her experience growing up as
biracial in America. Amelie spends her school year debating the world's foremost humanitarian issues
through her school's Model United Nations team, and spends her summers reading romance novels.

Leslie Lewinter grew up in a diverse immigrant community and, as she has often said, "It informed my life." After receiving her
graduate degree in Community Organization and Social Research, and marrying someone with the same perspective,
Leslie and her husband have lived and worked throughout the world, including Senegal, Thailand, Peru and the United States,
where Leslie directed an inner-city program for Lyndon Johnson's War on Poverty...taking her firstborn to work with her,
so she could mother and solve at the same time. Leslie has published books, including those on childhood malnutrition,
short stories in literary journals, and written satire for newspapers. She also has had plays produced, including the
award-winning A Revolutionary Mind, about the fates of two activists. But, Leslie will tell you that her greatest achievement
is her children, who help to make the world a better, more humane world.

About the illustrator

Maria Dmitrieva is an illustrator of children's books. She has wanted to be an illustrator for her entire life
and is thrilled to help authors bring their ideas to life. Maria has illustrated other books and drawn postcards,
after starting her career at an early age with custom portraits. Currently, she lives in
St. Petersburg - one of the most beautiful cities in Russia. Her hobbies include reading
books on psychology and watching movies.
You can follow her on Instagram at marrr_shine.

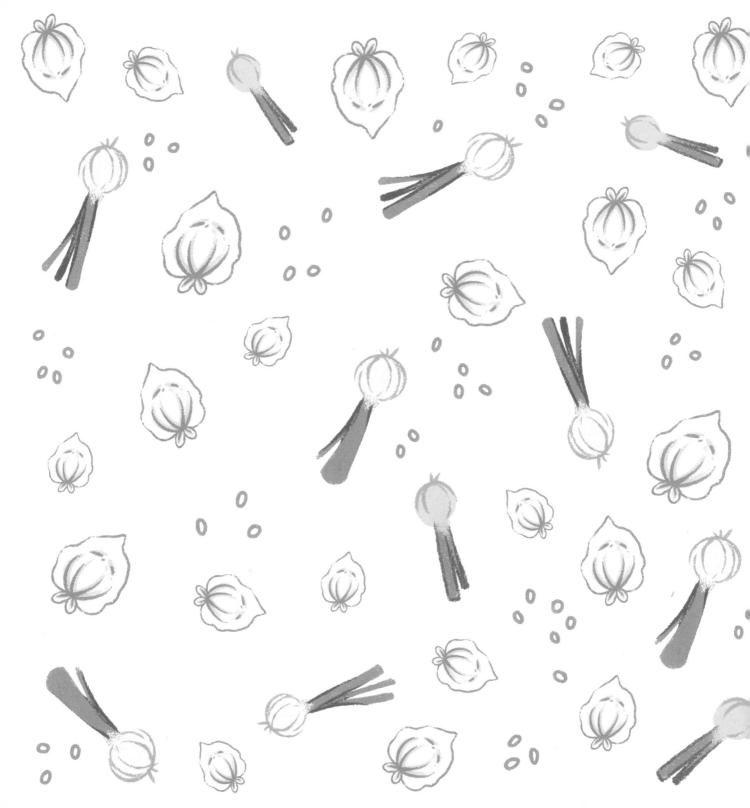

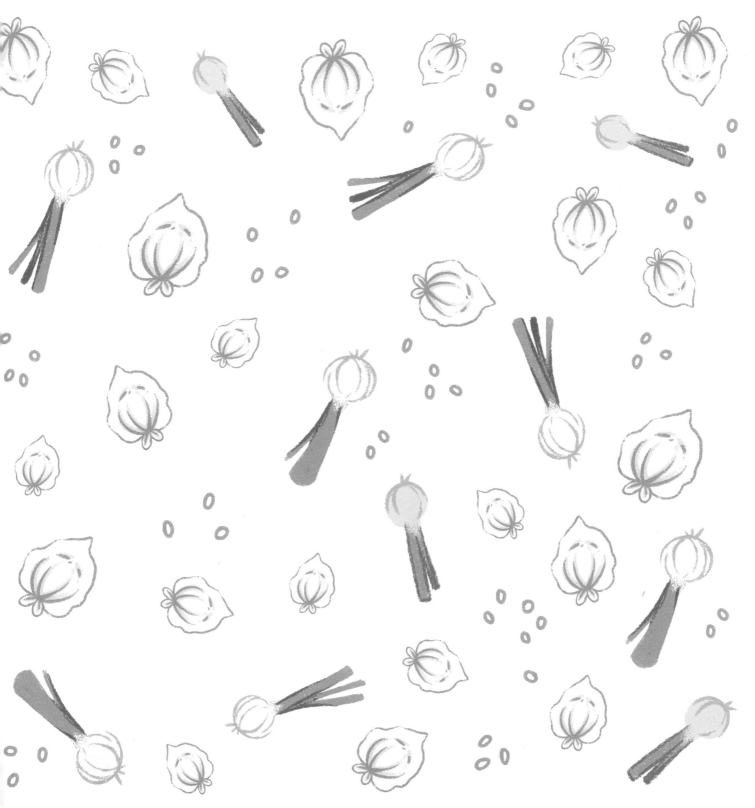